Eddie
Annie

I Can't
WA

AMY SCHWARTZ

BEACH LANE BOOKS • New York London Toronto Sydney New Delhi

For Leonard

An imprint of Simon & Schuster Children's Publishing Division
1230 Avenue of the Americas, New York, New York 10020

For information about special discounts for bulk purchases, please contact Simon & Schuster Special Sales at 1-866-506-1949 or business@simonandschuster.com.
The Simon & Schuster Speakers Bureau can bring authors to your live event. For more information or to book an event, contact the Simon & Schuster Speakers Bureau at 1-866-248-3049 or visit our website at www.simonspeakers.com.
Book design by Lauren Rille
The text for this book is set in Brandon Grotesque.
The illustrations for this book are rendered in gouache and pen and ink on Rives BFK.
Manufactured in China
0815 SCP
First Edition
10 9 8 7 6 5 4 3 2 1
Library of Congress Cataloging-in-Publication Data
Schwartz, Amy, author, illustrator.
I can't wait! / Amy Schwartz. — First edition.
pages cm
Summary: Neighbors William, Annie, and Thomas are all at their houses, each waiting for something very different and special.
ISBN 978-1-4424-8231-9 (hardcover) — ISBN 978-1-4424-8232-6 (ebook)
[1. Expectation (Psychology)—Fiction. 2. Family life—Fiction. 3. Friendship—Fiction.] I. Title. II. Title: I cannot wait!
PZ7.S406Iaae 2015
[E]—dc23
2013046543

Waiting

William was waiting
on his front stoop.

Annie was waiting
in her backyard.

And, in his house on the corner,
Thomas was waiting too.

William

A girl came skipping by William's front stoop.
"William," she said, "what are you doing?"
"I'm waiting," William said, "for something special."
"Are you waiting for a rabbit?"
"No," William said.
"Well, good-bye!" the girl said, and skipped on.

A boy ran by, chasing a ball.
"William," he said, "what are you doing?"
"I'm waiting," William said, "for something to hug."
"Is it a fat chubby baby with fat chubby cheeks
and fat chubby hands?"
"No," William said.
"Oh," the boy said, and ran on.

William's neighbor came by.
She put down her groceries.
"William," she said,
"what are you doing?"

"I'm waiting," William said,
"for something that's warm."

“Is it a fire-breathing dragon holding a princess
being rescued by a prince on a horse?”
“No,” William said.
“Oh. Well, I hope it comes soon.”
And William’s neighbor continued on home.

The mailman arrived with the mail.
"William," he said, "what are you doing?"
"I'm waiting," William said,
"for something amazing."
"Is it a chocolate fudge sundae
with peanuts and with whipped cream,
and with a cherry on top?"
"No," William said.
"It's *much* more amazing."
"Gracious!" the mailman said,
and went on his way.

A man with a mustache ran up William's steps with a skip and a hop.

"William," he said, "what are you doing?"

"I'm waiting," William said.

"Oh," the man said, "what are you waiting for?"

"Papa," William said, "I'm waiting for you!"
William's papa hugged William.
"I love you!" he said.
And William hugged his papa.
"Papa, I love you too!"

Annie

In her yard, Annie picked a dandelion.
She blew off the fuzz.
"Puppy," she said, "I wonder where Eddie is.
Is he getting a haircut? Is he eating a pickle?
Is he flying an airplane? Is he riding a train?
Puppy, where's Eddie? I thought we were friends."

"Puppy, did Eddie get a new kitten?
Or a bird?
Or a fish?
Did Eddie make a new friend?
Is she nicer than me?"

Annie pedaled her bike faster and faster.
"Where's Eddie?" Annie said.
"Why isn't he here yet?
Puppy," she said, "I think I know why."

"It's because I can't say my S's.
It's because my ears are so big.
It's because I have too many freckles.
It's because my hair is so red!"

Annie climbed up her ladder.

She slid down her slide.

"Puppy," she said, "on Tuesday,
I ate Eddie's grape Popsicle.
Then I ate all of his chips."

"I broke his new truck.
I lost his new ball."

"And that's why Eddie hates me!
I'm *not* his best friend!"

Annie heard a knock. She opened the gate.
"Annie," Eddie said, "I've been waiting and waiting!
I waited and waited, and then I went looking.
Are you hiding? Don't you like me?
Aren't we best friends?"

“Eddie,” Annie said, “you’ve been waiting for me?
I’ve been waiting for you!”
Annie gave Eddie a hug.
“Eddie,” she said, “you’re my very best,
most best,
always best friend!”

Thomas

In a big rocking chair, Thomas rocked with his grandma.
"Our new baby is coming," she said.
"Thomas, you're such a good helper.
Can you help think of a name?"
Thomas stopped rocking.
He started thinking right then.

Under the stairs,
Thomas played with his cat.
"Kitty," he said,
"for the baby, how's Fluffy?
Or Muffy?
Or Tiger?
Or Tabby?
Or Whiskers?
Or Snowball?
Or Spot?"

Outside, Thomas
watered his flowers.
"Kitty," he said,
"I like the name Daffodil."

"I like Violet Petunia.
I like Daisy Chrysanthemum.
I like Peony Rose."

In the kitchen, Grandma gave Thomas the spoon.
He took a big lick.

"Grandma," Thomas said,
"let's name our baby
Penelope.

Or Penelope Veronica,

or Penelope Isabelle,

or Penelope Annabelle,

or Penelope Clarabelle,

or Penelope . . .
Anne!"

Thomas waited with Grandma.
They waited, and waited,
and they waited some more.

They weeded the flowers.

They folded the laundry.

They gave Kitty her milk.

Then, the door opened.

Thomas's parents were home,

with his new baby brother.
And they all named him . . .

John!

William, Annie, and Thomas

Papa pulled William
to the park in his wagon.

Annie and Eddie pedaled to the park,
giggling and laughing.

Thomas skipped to the park,
chatting with Grandma.

"Hi, William!"
"Hi, Annie!"
"Hi, Thomas!"
"Meet my papa," William said.
"I was waiting for him."

"Meet Eddie," Annie said.
"He's my best friend. I was waiting for him."
"I have a new baby brother," Thomas said.
"You'll meet him soon. I was waiting for him."

Then the friends played together
until it was time to go home.

"Good-bye,"
William said.

"Good-bye,"
Eddie said.

"Good-bye,"
Annie said.

"Good-bye," Thomas said.
"Let's play again tomorrow."

“Yes,” William said.

“I can’t wait!”

William
Thomas